the
night before
Christmas
in Utah

Sue Carabine

Illustrations by

Sherry Meenon Kawasaki

05 04 03 02   6 5 4 3
Copyright © 2000 by Gibbs Smith, Publisher

Published by
Gibbs Smith, Publisher
P.O. Box 667
Layton, Utah 84041

Orders: (1-800) 748-5439
E-mail: *info@gibbs-smith.com*
Website: *www.gibbs-smith.com*

Designed and produced by
    Mary Ellen Thompson, TTA Design
Printed in China

ISBN 0-87905-981-8

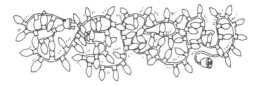

'Twas the night before Christmas
in the great Beehive State,
St. Nick and his reindeer—
they just couldn't wait.

They'd flown over Provo
and Mount Timpanogos,
Watched Navajo children
hang moccasins in hogans.

Nick also spied Zion and
Bryce National Parks,
Then zoomed over Moab
and through Delicate Arch.

"Season's Greetings to Utah,"
he chuckled with glee,
"This is one of our most
favorite places to be!"

On Bonneville Salt Flats,
the record he'd broken;
Then buzzing Great Salt Lake,
he truly was smokin'!

When all of a sudden
he heard a loud crack,
And the sleigh started falling
along with his sack!

Dasher and team tried
to regain control,
But the sleigh and dear Santa
went into a roll!

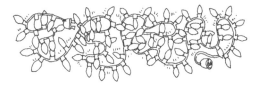

"Something hit us," he roared,
"and we're gonna get wet!
Was it a missile that sped by
or was it a jet?!"

Before they could answer,
a saltwatery splash
Covered reindeer, St. Nicholas,
and all of his stash!

Well, the lake is so buoyant
that nothing can sink,
So they floated together,
Nick trying to think.

The dripping wet sleigh
looked just like a boat,
While Nick sat embarrassed
in a soggy red coat!

Then soldiers from Dugway
picked up old St. Nick
And calmed down the reindeer,
who were getting seasick!

The GIs looked sheepish
and not a bit jolly,
"Say, Santa," they said,
"we really are sorry,

"But you flew over Tooele
and came in so low,
That our radar suggested
an armed UFO.

"So we fired a missile
that quickly gave chase;
It's too bad, old-timer,
you were in our air space."

When hearing these words
Nick got really upset,
"No one has called me
an old-timer yet."

His face grew quite red
and his eyes lost their twinkle
And his fat little nose
soon started to wrinkle.

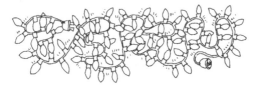

"Well, maybe we'll leave;
we can see we're not wanted.
Try Christmas without us,"
his reindeer then taunted.

"Oh no!" the guys pleaded,
"now look what we did!
Just how will we ever
explain to our kids?"

Though Santa was joking,
he'd keep these guys guessing;
He was *not* an "old-timer"
And he'd teach them a lesson!

"Well, I guess if you're sorry,
you just might want to parley;
Go ask Karl Malone
if I can ride on his Harley.

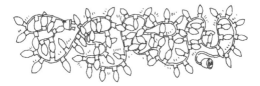

"And, wait! while you're there,
see what tickets he has
For me and my reindeer—
front seats for the Jazz!"

Those GIs sure moved fast,
the word got out quick,
Karl appeared on his cycle,
prepared for St. Nick!

"Climb up behind me,
old-t . . . , uh, Santa," he cried.
"No, *you* behind *me*,"
quipped St. Nicholas with pride.

So that's how it was,
while Karl howled, "No! No!"
Nick roared up the Wasatch
with a jolly "Ho! Ho!"

When they halted, Karl murmured,
"I'm done with that cycle.
Just take it, please, Santa,
and ride it with Michael!"

Santa waved a farewell
while shaking with mirth,
Said, "I've heard talk about
'The Greatest Snow on Earth.'

"At Winter Sports Park
they've built something quite huge;
My reindeer and I should
try out that smooth luge!"

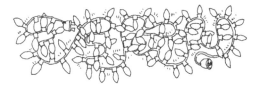

Well, Comet and Cupid,
eyes wide with dark fears,
Knew Donner and Blitzen
would land on their rears.

Still, Santa insisted,
his round face just beaming
As they ALL rode the luge,
his deer kicking and screaming!

"Are we just about done here?
The kids are in bed,"
Asked the soldiers, quite frantic.
"Don't worry," Nick said.

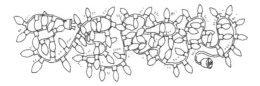

"We *old-timers* are clever,"
then added in haste,
"But, I'll need an F-16
from Hill Air Force Base!"

The reindeer all heard this,
then huddled in shock,
Till Santa said, "Quit that,
and go for a walk.

"I'll do this myself,
I can fly with perfection."
Eyes twinkling, he added,
"There's always ejection!"

So up St. Nick roared,
then looked down with great care:
"At Christmas, there's nothing
quite like Temple Square!"

As lights sparkled brightly
on each shrub and tree,
He softly said, "These folks
know it's not about me!"

When Santa returned
from his flight in the jet,
He had to replace
all the gifts that got wet.

So he rode on the Trax
and shopped at the malls
Where he got what he needed:
kids' toys, games, and all!

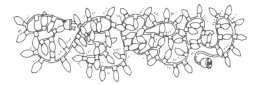

Now Santa's quite proud of his
crack reindeer team,
And he knows they can win
on the rodeo scene.

So for Pioneer Days
he would register now,
And get back in July to
Days of '47 somehow!

He then asked the soldiers
to open Lagoon,
Where all rode the rides—
it was over too soon!

The Rocket, Colossus,
and huge Ferris Wheel,
They had to themselves.
My! What a cool deal!

At last St. Nick came to
his final request:
A grand invitation to
appear as a guest

And sing just one song with
the Tabernacle Choir.
He enlisted the soldiers
to obtain his desire.

They promised they would,
and delivered on cue;
Excited, Nick spruced up
with everything new.

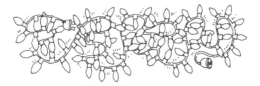

From State to West Temple,
he strode briskly along;
Anticipating his venture,
he broke into song:

"Jolly Old St. Nich-o-las, . . ."
he chuckled with glee,
"I know we'll sing that one;
it's all about me!"

Well, that's just what happened
(old Santa sang bass);
All joyously recalled
that big grin on his face!

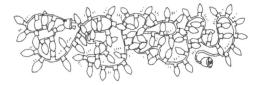

And so, on this note,
Santa said his good-byes
To dear friends in Utah,
he waved from the skies,

Calling, "This IS the place,
a most wonderful sight!
Merry Christmas, dear Utah,
to all a Good Night!"